This Ladybird book belongs to

....

BUS
STOP

For Ruth – P.M.

For Olive – T.N.

LADYBIRD BOOKS

UK | USA | Canada | Ireland | Australia
India | New Zealand | South Africa

Ladybird Books is part of the Penguin Random House group of companies
whose addresses can be found at global.penguinrandomhouse.com.

www.penguin.co.uk www.puffin.co.uk www.ladybird.co.uk

First published 2022
001

Written by Peter Millett
Illustrated by Tony Neal

Printed in China

The authorized representative in the EEA is Penguin Random House Ireland,
Morrison Chambers, 32 Nassau Street, Dublin D02 YH68

A CIP catalogue record for this book is available from the British Library

ISBN: 978–0–241–49368–7

All correspondence to:
Ladybird Books, Penguin Random House Children's
One Embassy Gardens, 8 Viaduct Gardens, London SW11 7BW

THE PIRATES ON THE BUS

Written by
PETER MILLETT

Illustrated by
TONY NEAL

The pirates on the bus go,

"Yo ho ho!

Yo ho ho!

Yo ho ho!"

The pirates on the bus go,

"Yo

All through
the land.

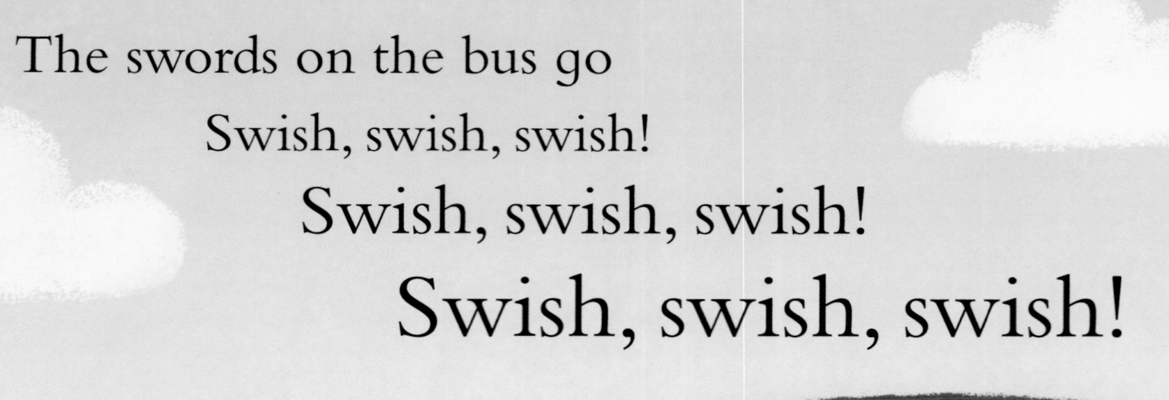

The swords on the bus go

Swish, swish, swish!

Swish, swish, swish!

Swish, swish, swish!

The swords on the bus go

Swish, swish, swish!

All through the land.

The bosun on the bus goes,

"Thar she blows!

Thar she blows!

Thar she blows!"

The bosun on the bus goes,

"Thar she blows!"

All through the land.

The captain on the bus goes,
"Find the gold!
Find the gold!
Find the gold!"

The captain on the bus goes,

All through the land.

The pirates on the bus go

Jump,
jump,
jump!

Jump,
jump,
jump!

Jump,
jump,
jump!

The pirates on the bus go

Jump, jump, jump!

Deep in the sand.

The captain and her crew go

Dig, dig, dig!

Dig, dig, dig!

Dig, dig, dig!

The captain and her crew go

Dig,

dig,
dig!
Under
the sand.

The treasure in the chest goes

Clink, clink, clink!

Clink, clink, clink!

Clink, clink, clink!

The treasure in the chest goes

Clink,

clink,

clink!

All on the sand.

The parrot on the bus squawks,

"Back on board!

Back on board!

Back on board!"

The parrot on the bus squawks,

All on the sand.

The wheels on the bus go

Down, down, down!

Down, down, down!

Down, down, down!

The wheels on the bus go

Down, down, down!

Deep in
the sand.

The captain on the bus goes,

"Clear the decks!

Clear the decks!

Clear the decks!"

The captain on the bus goes,

All on the sand.

The crew on the beach go,

"Heave and ho!

Heave and ho!

Heave and ho!"

The crew on the beach go,

All on the sand.

The pirates in their bunks go
Swing and sway,
Swing and sway,
Swing and sway!

The pirates in their bunks go

Swing
and sway!
All the way home!

BUS
STOP

Look out for more Ladybird picture books . . .

ISBN: 9780241493618 ☐

ISBN: 9780241473085 ☐

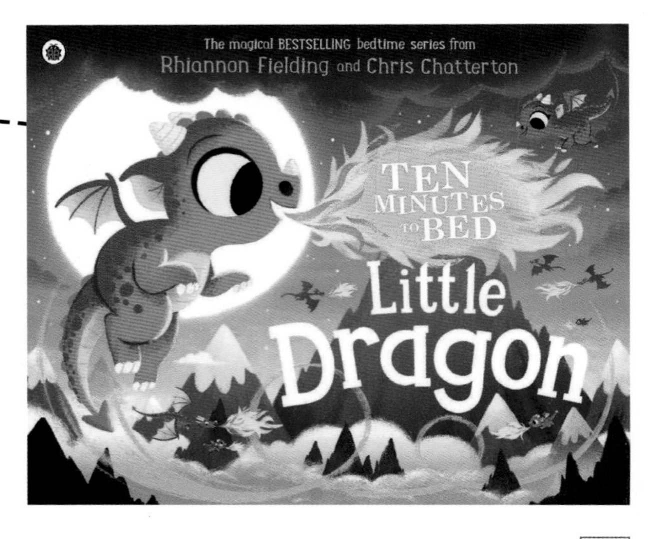

ISBN: 9780241464373 ☐

ISBN: 9780241407929 ☐

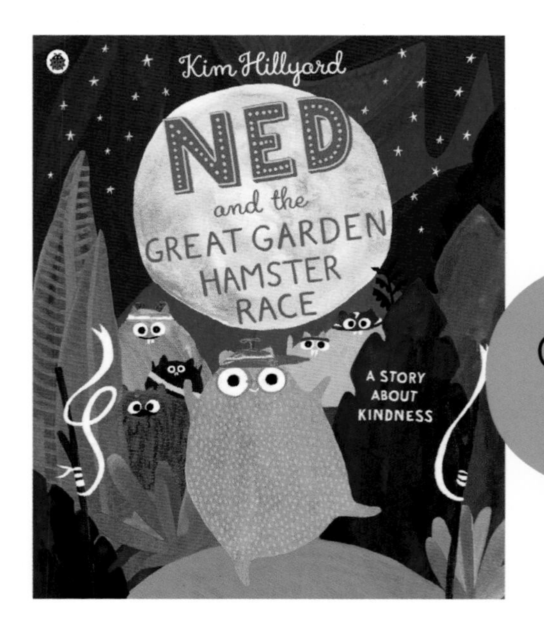

ISBN: 9780241413418 ☐

Can you collect them all?